P9-DTB-664

RECEIVED
JAN 0 6 2023
By

NO LONGER PROPERTY OF
SEATTLE PUBLIC LIBRARY

Trouble at the Paw Park

Read More
Trillium Sisters
Stories!

Trillium Sisters

Trouble at the Paw Park

Laura Brown and Elly Kramer
Illustrated by Sarah Mensinga

PIXEL✛INK

PIXEL✚INK

Text copyright © 2022 by Laura Brown and Elly Kramer

All illustrations copyright © 2022 by TGM Development Corp.

All rights reserved

Pixel+Ink is an imprint of TGM Development Corp.

www.pixelandinkbooks.com

Printed and bound in September 2022 at Thomson Reuters, Eagan, MN, U.S.A.

Book design by Yaffa Jaskoll

Cataloging-in-Publication information is available from the Library of Congress.

Hardcover ISBN: 978-1-64595-066-0

Paperback ISBN: 978-1-64595-067-7

E-book ISBN: 978-1-64595-104-9

First Edition

1 3 5 7 9 10 8 6 4 2

For Mary Harrington and Bethany Buck,
who believed in this series from
day one. Your support has been our
super power. Thank you!
—L.B. and E.K.

CHAPTER 1

Emmy smiled as she took a step back from the sign. "Welcome to the Paw Park," she read aloud.

"Great name, sis!" Giselle exclaimed. Then she hopped down the stairs to enter the underground park.

Clare, their other sister, followed. "Em, this place looks trillsome!"

Emmy grinned. She and her father had been working on the animal park all summer.

It was completely below ground, but it was so bright that bushes, flowers, and even some small trees grew up through the dirt floor. It was connected to the Paw *Pad*, their father's pet clinic, by a set of stairs.

"I've never seen anything like it," said Giselle. "How'd you and Dad dream this up?"

"Well," Emmy began, "it was one of those super-hot days on the mountain. The animals were resting in the shade, but it didn't help. Poor Bruce the Moose kept wading into the pond to cool off."

Clare gave a sympathetic nod. "Summers keep getting hotter and hotter."

"Yup," said Emmy. "So we were brainstorming how to help the animals."

"I remember! You and Dad were at the

kitchen table for hours. You drank all the daisy juice," Clare teased.

Emmy laughed. "Sorry about that! Anyway, since it's naturally cool underground, we figured a below-ground park would be a great addition to the clinic. Clients can easily bring their pets here for exercise."

"Yeah, but how'd you make it so bright and sunny down here?" asked Clare.

"We put devices on the roof that capture sunlight and channel it underground," said Emmy. "Then we added this special ceiling that spreads that sunshine around."

Clare tilted her head. The ceiling had shiny tiles that looked almost like mirrors all over it.

Suddenly they heard a "*Yip, yip!*" as their

eaglet, Soar, flew across the park. Claw, their bear cub, and Fluffy, their wolf pup, chased after her.

"The mini'mals love it here! Your mission is accomplished, Em," said Giselle.

Emmy skipped toward the stairs. "Let's go, I can't wait for the other pets to arrive!"

"It's gonna be a hoot," agreed Clare. "I'm so excited for your grand opening!"

But before they could head upstairs, their father called down to them.

"Trills, are you in the park?" Dr. J.A. called. *Trills* was the sisters' nickname, short for *trillium*, their favorite flower. With three leaves, the trillium was a triplet, just like they were.

"The minis are checking it out, Dad," Emmy answered.

"And they love it!" added Clare.

As their father climbed down and stepped inside, Claw welcomed him. *"Ahoo!"*

"Wow. Everything looks great! Are we ready?" he asked.

"We sure are," answered Emmy.

"Then let's welcome our furry guests!" their dad said.

CHAPTER 2

Just as Emmy was about to race upstairs, Dr. J.A.'s phone rang. She waited as her father spoke. "That doesn't sound good."

"What's going on?" Giselle mouthed to her sisters.

Clare shrugged. "No clue."

"On my way," Dr. J.A. said as he hung up. "Trills, that was Mayor Mae. The aspens in Aspen Grove have dead branches, and sap oozing from the bark. Those are signs of illness. I've got to get over there."

"But what about the Paw Park, Dad? It's our first day," said Emmy.

"I know, honey," he said softly. "And I'm excited, but I can't turn my back on sick aspens. Trees clean the air we breathe and make the temperature cooler."

"Plus, animals and birds live in the trees," Clare added.

Emmy looked down. *I know Dad has to help the aspens. But we worked so hard to create the Paw Park together. All the pets are waiting to be let in!*

It was as if her father read her mind. "Just because I can't stay, doesn't mean you have to postpone opening day."

Emmy looked at her dad. "You mean open the Paw Park without you? How?"

"Em," began Dr. J.A., "you've been helping at the clinic for a year now. You already take care of the pets when I have to go out."

"But I've never taken care of that many all by myself," noted Emmy.

Dr. J.A. winked at Giselle and Clare. "I think you may be able to find some helpers."

"Would you, Trills?" asked Emmy.

"Em, do you even have to ask?" Giselle teased. "Remember, teamwork—"

"Makes the dream work!" finished Clare.

Emmy smiled. "So, Dad, are you saying what I think you're saying?"

Giselle jumped to her feet. "And what I'm thinking!"

Clare opened her eyes wide. "Dad, is Emmy *in charge* of the Paw Park today?"

"As long as you three work together, it's a *paws*itively perfect plan!" he said.

Emmy clapped her hands. "Thanks, Dad!"

"Thank *you*, girls. Now, before I go, let's review what you need to do," said Dr. J.A.

Clare handed Emmy the notebook she carried to jot down ideas. "You got this, sis."

Emmy got ready to write.

CHAPTER 3

"Okay, I think I have it," Emmy said. She read the list back to be sure. "First, let all the pets exercise in the Paw Park. Then, give them a snack. Next, it's naptime. And last, bathe them before pickup."

"Perfect," said Dr. J.A.

Clare stood up. "So, are we ready to open?"

"Yup," said Dr. J.A. as he threw his pack over his shoulder. "And don't forget. Mrs.

Lilienstern is watching your little brother. She's a call away if you need any help."

"Poor little bro, missing all the action," sighed Giselle.

"Zee loves Mrs. Lilienstern. She crafts with him," said their father. "Plus, he'll be here later to celebrate opening day. And if I hurry, I will be, too."

As Emmy hugged her father goodbye, her stomach did a little flip-flop. She couldn't wait to watch the pets enjoy the Paw Park. But it was a big responsibility to take care of so many animals. She wanted to make her father proud.

"One last thing. Trills, drumroll please," said Dr. J.A. Clare and Giselle drummed their knees with their hands. Dr. J.A. dug into his pocket and pulled out something shiny. He pressed it into Emmy's palm. "For the keeper of the Paw Park!"

Emmy opened her hand and gasped. "My own key? Wow!"

"You can't be in charge if you can't get in and out of here," laughed Dr. J.A.

"Thanks, Dad. I will be

super careful with this." Clare, who always had craft supplies with her, grabbed a green ribbon from her pocket and laced it through the key. Then she hung it around Emmy's neck, just below the green trillium petal charm she always wore.

Giselle gave her a high five. "Looking good, sis."

"The Paw Park is in good hands. I mean paws," Dr. J.A. teased. He laughed at his own joke, then scooted up the steps and headed out to Aspen Grove.

CHAPTER 4

Emmy made her way to the front door. She took a deep breath and threw it open. "Hi everyone and thank you for coming! We are *trilled* your pets want to try the Paw Park, our new underground addition! Please follow me, and be careful on the stairs."

"*Ahoo!*"

"*Ruff, ruff!*"

"*Squeak!*"

The animals were so excited, they made a racket as the group descended the stairs. When they finally arrived at the park entrance, the customers all clapped. Emmy smiled from ear to ear.

"This park is gorgeous. It's like being outside but we're inside!" Mr. Connor, the owner of Shakey Shakes, said. He handed his bunny, Harry, to Giselle, who set him gently on the grass. Harry immediately hopped away. "Guess Harry likes it, too. Well done! You girls should come by for celebratory milkshakes!"

"We'd love to! When we're not pet sitting," agreed Giselle.

Next in line was Miss Amaya, the town librarian. She held Peter, her friendly pika in one arm, and her book bag in the other.

"Awww, I just love pikas," Clare cooed. "They remind me of hamsters."

Peter wriggled so much, Miss Amaya almost dropped him.

"Here, let me help," said Clare. She took Peter and put him down so he could race after Harry.

Miss Amaya breathed a sigh of relief, and rested her book on the grass. "Thank you, Clare. Peter can be a handful, and my arms got tired."

Next was Mrs. Heartlove, their neighbor. She placed Chad the chipmunk in Emmy's hands. "This guy needs more exercise than I can provide. Thank goodness you girls opened this park!"

"Glad to help," Emmy called as she carried Chad toward the bushes and set him down. She smiled as he darted in and out of them. The mini'mals were super gentle with other animals, and followed the little ones to look after them.

Emmy returned to the entrance of the Paw Park, where Giselle was filling water bowls for the pets. In a corner, Mr. Connor, Miss Amaya, and Mrs. Heartlove were deep in conversation. It didn't seem like they were simply chitchatting.

Clare stood near the adults. She pretended to examine the blueberry bush. "Clare, what are you doing? Giselle needs help with the water bowls," said Emmy.

But Clare didn't move. "Clare—"

"Shh," whispered Clare. "I can't hear the grown-ups if you're talking." She leaned in their direction.

"Clare, are you eaves-dropping?" whispered Emmy. "Dad wouldn't like that."

"I know. But the adults seem upset. I'm trying to figure out why," Clare said in a low voice.

Emmy touched the green trillium petal charm in her necklace at the mention of *upset*. Each of the girls had a charm that could combine with the others in an emergency to grant them magic powers. Though their powers were incredible, Emmy hoped they wouldn't need magic today. More than anything, she just wanted opening day to go smoothly.

Giselle trotted over. "What's up?"

"Shhh!" her sisters both hissed.

That's when they heard Mr. Connor raise his voice. He sounded alarmed. "I *know*! It's the strangest thing!"

"I just can't figure out what happened," Miss

Amaya complained.

"I would like to know who's responsible!" Mrs. Heartlove added. She shook her head. Then she said something softer that the girls couldn't hear.

Giselle took Clare's hand. "Sis, this is silly. If you want to know what's wrong, let's just ask." She pulled her sister toward the adults.

CHAPTER 5

"Hi, there," Giselle said. "We couldn't help but notice that you seem a little worried. Is there anything we can do?"

"We're good at helping," Emmy added.

"We know, dear," Miss Amaya said. "But you have your hands full with the animals."

Mr. Connor gave her a look. "Maybe they know something. Let's tell them what happened."

That's all Mrs. Heartlove needed to hear. "Girls, there has been some very mysterious activity in Trillville."

Giselle raised an eyebrow. "Mysterious?"

"Things around the village have gone missing," Ms. Amaya added.

"Like what?" Giselle pressed.

Mrs. Heartlove dropped her voice to a whisper. "Well for starters, when I woke up this morning, the lightbulbs from my porch lights were gone!"

"That *is* weird," agreed Clare.

"And dangerous," continued their neighbor. "My front porch is going to be dark tonight!"

"Don't worry," said Miss Amaya as she wrapped an arm around her. "We'll replace the lightbulbs before it gets dark."

"It gets stranger," Mr. Connor chimed in. "My doorbell rang last night and then again this morning, but when I opened the door both times, no one was there!"

"Was a package delivered?" wondered Emmy.

"Nope," answered Mr. Connor.

"Huh," mused Clare. "Doorbells don't ring on their own. Anything else?"

"The covers to my trash bins disappeared! And there's litter all over my yard!" added Miss Amaya.

"That could have been the wind. The tops blow off our bins all the time," offered Emmy.

"But mine were strapped down," explained Miss Amaya.

"There *must* be a logical explanation for all of this," said Giselle.

"We'll think on it," added Clare.

The girls liked to be helpful, and take care of their neighbors.

"Thanks, girls. Let us know if you come up with anything," said Miss Amaya.

"And take good care of the pets! We'll see you later," added Mr. Connor. The grown-ups headed for the stairs.

Clare furrowed her brow. Something didn't look right. That's when she noticed Miss Amaya's book bag was still on the grass. "Wait, your bag!"

Miss Amaya turned back. "Oh, I'd be lost without that. You have an eye for detail, my dear. Thank you."

"Clare notices everything," agreed Giselle. "She's like a detective."

"What a gift," said Mr. Connor. He smiled at the grown-ups. "Now ladies, can I treat you to a coffee shake at the shop?"

"We thought you'd never ask," said Mrs. Heartlove. With that, the adults climbed the stairs and headed for town.

CHAPTER 6

Clare turned to her sisters when they were alone. "Maybe we should check out where the neighbors' stuff went missing. There might be some clues as to what happened."

"That would be super helpful," agreed Giselle. "What do you think, Em?"

"Umm, I don't know. Dad put me in charge of the pets. I think we need to stay here."

Clare picked up the notebook and pointed to their list. "Em, look. The first thing was to exercise the pets. We've done that already."

Emmy looked around. The park was strangely quiet. "Trills, where *are* the pets?"

"They're playing, Em. Let's find them," said Clare.

Emmy found Peter pika under a zucchini leaf. He was tuckered out from all the exercise. "Don't fall asleep before snack time, Peter," she said as she scooped him up.

Clare spotted Harry the bunny digging a hole to rest in. "That's not where you're napping today, sweetie." She carried him in the crook of her arm.

Chad the chipmunk was skittering down a path, chasing Claw and Fluffy. Giselle whistled to the pets, and they followed her toward the entrance, with Chad trailing behind.

"Phew! I'm glad we found them," said Emmy. "But that's my point. As much as I'd like to help the grown-ups, our job is to take care of the pets today."

"You're right, Em. We should have noticed they were getting tired," agreed Clare.

"No harm done," Emmy noted. "Now, let's get these cuties some water and a snack."

Upstairs in the clinic, the girls set out bowls of fresh water, and each pet got a special treat. Then the girls settled Harry, Peter, and Chad in cages for naps. The little critters were asleep before their fur hit the pillows!

Meanwhile, the mini'mals were still full

of energy and headed back down to the Paw Park for more playtime.

Giselle drummed her fingers on her thigh. Her other leg bounced restlessly. "There's nothing to do while the little pets are sleeping."

"Maybe we could visit where the stuff went missing *now*," Clare suggested.

"I don't know. What if the pets wake up while we're gone?" asked Emmy.

Giselle grabbed the Pet Cam, a baby monitor their father used to check on pets when he was away from the clinic. "We can take the cam. If we see anything wrong, we'll run right back."

Emmy looked from her sisters to the sleeping pets. "Dad *does* leave the pets alone sometimes. . . ."

Giselle and Clare nodded in agreement.

Emmy shifted from foot to foot. What would her dad do? *He left the Paw Park to help the aspens. Maybe he'd want me to help our neighbors.*

"Okay, let's do it," Emmy agreed.

CHAPTER 7

"Gang!" Clare whooped. "I may or may not have found this in the clinic!" She held up a magnifying glass. "Dad uses it to search for ticks on the animals, but it will help us find clues, too."

"Clues?" said Emmy.

"Ya know, to solve the mystery of who took our neighbors' stuff!" Clare replied.

Giselle giggled. "I told the grown-ups you were like a detective, Clare!"

Clare held the magnifying glass to her eye. "Inspector Clare, at your service!"

Emmy grabbed some human snacks from Dad's supply and stuffed them into her backpack. "In case we get hungry when we're on the case."

The girls ran downstairs to get the mini'mals. They needed a lot more exercise than the clients' pets, so the girls decided to take them along. Clare settled Fluffy into her pack and swung it onto her back. Soar flew to Giselle's shoulder, her favorite perch, while Emmy settled Claw into the bear wrap she wore cross body. Then they tiptoed up the steps so as not to wake the other pets and slipped outside.

"Trills, let's solve this mystery," said Clare.

Emmy felt her tummy flip-flop for the second time that day, like it had done earlier when her father put her in charge of the Paw Park. Why was she worried, when her sisters seemed so calm? They had taken good care of the pets, and now they were going to help their owners. She took a deep breath as she removed the key from around her neck and locked the door to the clinic, pressing the handle twice to make sure it was secure. *Check and check!* With one last nervous glance, she joined her sisters.

CHAPTER 8

"Where to first?" Giselle asked.

"I'm thinking we start at Mrs. Heartlove's front porch," Clare answered.

"Agree," said Emmy. "Mrs. Heartlove was really upset. We should help her first."

When they arrived, the girls examined the light fixtures.

"Nothing looks wrong—except that the lightbulbs are missing," Giselle observed.

Clare searched the porch and the yard. "No clues as to who was here!"

"I don't get it," Emmy said. "Lightbulbs don't just disappear. Where do you think they went?"

"It looks tricky to get those bulbs out of the fixtures," Giselle noted. "So, it must have been a grown-up."

"But why would someone take lightbulbs?" asked Emmy.

"Maybe the person ran out and borrowed a bulb?" Giselle offered.

"But wouldn't they have asked or at least left a note?" Emmy replied.

"Maybe it was a kid who took the light-bulbs as a funny prank?" Clare said.

Giselle frowned. "That's not funny. Mrs.

Heartlove could trip in the dark."

"But it does make sense. Remember Mr. Connor's doorbell rang, and no one was there? That also sounds like a prank," Emmy added.

"Yeah, let's head over there next," Giselle suggested.

"Hopefully Mr. Connor's house will shed some light on the situation!" Clare joked.

CHAPTER 9

When they arrived at Mr. Connor's house, Giselle grabbed the magnifying glass from Clare's pack. "He said that the doorbell rang last night and again this morning. I'll take a good look at the bell for clues."

"Anything?" Emmy asked hopefully.

"Nothing," Giselle answered after carefully inspecting the mechanism.

Clare stood in the yard. "This is strange,

Trills. The ground is muddy, but I don't see any footprints. If a kid rang the bell, their sneakers would have left a mark. How did they get to the front door?"

"No idea," said Giselle.

"I'm not convinced this was all a prank," Emmy said. "Taking someone's lightbulbs isn't funny, it's dangerous."

The girls stood quietly. Even the minis seemed to be thinking.

Clare finally spoke. "There's only one thing to do. To the trash cans!"

"To the trash cans," Emmy and Giselle giggled.

CHAPTER 10

"Aroo!" Fluffy wiggled in the backpack as the sisters headed to Miss Amaya's tree house.

"I hear ya, boy," Clare said. "Trills, what do you think about letting the minis out for a bit? Fluffy is restless."

"Sure," Emmy agreed.

As soon as he was free, Fluffy put his nose to the ground and took off.

"Whoa, wait up, boy!" Clare called. Fluffy

raced toward several trash cans in the distance. All were missing their lids. Trash littered the yard.

"The thief had a feast!" observed Giselle. "There's not one smidge of food left on any of this trash. Just bones, and wrappers licked clean."

"Hmm," said Clare. "These clues suggest our thief is not human. A person might have dumped out the trash as a prank, but that's about it."

Emmy examined the shiny metal cans and noticed the straps that hung down from them, each with a hook attached to it. "Check this out, Trills. These straps go over the lid and hook to the other side of the can to keep it on tight."

"Well the straps sure didn't hold *these* lids on!" Clare pointed out. "Em, could an *animal* unhook a strap like that?"

"It's possible. Some animals use their paws almost like hands!"

Just then, Miss Amaya walked down her front steps and met the girls in the yard. "Trills, I didn't expect to see you here."

Giselle took out the Pet Cam and switched it on. "The pets are napping, see? We figured we'd see if we could find any clues to help you."

"Oh, thank you," replied Miss Amaya. "I left the trash on the lawn so you could see the evidence. Have you figured out who made this mess?"

"Not yet," said Clare.

"Well this might help. I forgot to mention I heard a hissing noise last night, through my open window," noted Miss Amaya.

"That confirms it," said Clare. "The clues point to an animal."

The girls helped Miss Amaya clean up, but they continued to think as they worked. "An animal might have gotten into the garbage, but it couldn't have unscrewed Mrs. Heartlove's lightbulbs or rung Mr. Connor's doorbell," Giselle mused.

"Plus, there were no prints of any kind in the mud in Mr. Connor's yard," Clare added.

"We must have missed something," Emmy concluded.

"Then what are we waiting for?" Giselle asked. "Back to the doorbell!"

CHAPTER 11

"Do you hear that?" Emmy asked as they approached Mr. Connor's porch.

Giselle nodded. "I do!"

"It sounds like the doorbell!" Clare exclaimed.

The girls raced to the front door, but when they arrived there was no one there. "This is nuts! How can a doorbell ring without anyone pressing the button?" wondered Emmy.

"Look!" Clare pointed to wires that ran from the doorbell into the wall.

"Oh," said Giselle. "I didn't see them before."

Emmy explained, "They make the doorbell ring when you press the button. Usually, they are completely in the wall so you don't see them."

"I need a closer look," said Clare.

Giselle pulled the magnifying glass out of the pack and handed it to her.

"Here's the problem!" gasped Clare. "There are teeth marks. Something chewed on the wires and damaged them. That's why the bell is ringing on its own."

"So, an animal is responsible for this *and* the trash cans," said Emmy.

"But what about the lightbulbs? An animal couldn't unscrew those, right?" asked Giselle.

"Don't be so sure. Some animals are so handy with their paws, they can do human-like things," answered Emmy.

"Huh," said Giselle. "You learn something new every day."

CHAPTER 12

They went to the edge of Mr. Connor's lawn to think about this new piece of information, when they heard a soft gurgle.

"What was that?" whispered Emmy.

"Another clue?" wondered Clare.

"Nope. Just my stomach," laughed Giselle. "We were so busy, we forgot to have a snack ourselves. I'm starving!"

"So am I come to think of it," said Clare.

The girls dropped their packs and sat in the grass. The minis lounged nearby.

"Ah, better," said Clare as she stretched her arms above her head. "The straps were digging into me." She reached into her pack and passed out snacks.

Emmy touched the key for the clinic. "This ribbon is cutting into my neck, too. I'm going to take it off and put it with your stuff while we rest." She laid the key necklace carefully on top of Clare's backpack.

Giselle tipped her head to the sun. "That feels so good, I could take a nap."

Emmy sat straight up. "*De bets*!!" she cried through a mouthful of granola.

"Huh?" asked Clare.

Emmy swallowed. "The pets. We didn't

really check on them when we were at Miss Amaya's. Gosh, I hope they're still sleeping. Hand me the Pet Cam, quick."

Clare dumped her backpack upside down onto the grass. "Don't worry, Em. I'm sure the animals are fine." She pulled the camera out and switched it on.

In a flash, the girls were able to see the pets still safe in their cages. But naptime was definitely over! Harry the bunny was sniffing around his cage. Every so often, he would hop up and down, rattling the metal cage against the counter and startling little Chad. Meanwhile, Peter pika was gnawing on the metal bars. Emmy knew it was a natural thing to do, and that Peter couldn't chew through them, but she *was* supposed to be caring for these critters. She had to get back.

"Trills, I'm going back to the Paw Park. The animals need me."

"But our neighbors need help, too," said Giselle.

Emmy thought for a moment. "We have to figure out what kind of animal can open trash cans and unscrew lightbulbs. And maybe likes to chew on things. I'll do some research back at the clinic. Meanwhile, you all take one last look for clues here."

"Good plan, sis," agreed Giselle.

"See you back there," said Clare.

With that, Emmy scooped up Claw and jogged toward the Paw Park.

CHAPTER 13

When Emmy was gone, Clare furrowed her brow in concentration. "We're so close. Let's think. What kind of animal likes trash *and* light-bulbs?" wondered Clare.

"Dunno," Giselle said as she paced.

"Sis, sit down. I can't think straight when you're bouncing around like that," said Clare.

"I think better when I move," responded Giselle.

Clare turned her back to her sister so she could focus. And that's when she saw it, on the other side of Mr. Connor's property, where it was ringed with close-knit bushes and woods. In one small spot, a bush looked crushed, like something had run through the foliage. "Giselle, over there! C'mon!" Giselle followed Clare to the the bush and together, they crouched to examine the ground around it.

"Are those tracks?" asked Giselle.

"I think so," said Clare. "But I wish Emmy were here. She's the expert on this."

"It almost looks human. Like five fingers or toes made this print," observed Giselle.

"We've gotta show this to Em—" began Clare, but she was interrupted by a *hiiissss* coming from the woods.

The hair on Fluffy's back stood straight up.

"Clare, do you hear that?" whispered Giselle.

"Miss Amaya said there was a hissing noise near her window last night."

"Yup. I remember. And that does *not* sound friendly. Come on." Clare grabbed her sister's hand, and they ran back to where they had been sitting. And that's when they saw it. A flash of brown fur streaked across the lawn ahead of them toward their things. Whatever animal it was snagged something from the grass in its mouth and kept going into the woods on the opposite side.

"Wow!" gasped Giselle.

"What'd it take?" asked Clare. "Granola bars?"

The girls raced to their belongings.

CHAPTER 14

Emmy had almost made it to the clinic when her hand flew to her chest and she stopped short. *The key! Aww, pine cones! I forgot to put it back around my neck when I left!*

Emmy called to Claw, who was ahead on the path.

"Ahoo?" The little bear knew something was wrong. Claw scampered to her.

"I forgot my key," said Emmy in a shaky

voice. "What am I going to do? I need to get to the animals!" Claw nuzzled Emmy's legs. "Let's go back to Claire and Giselle. Hopefully, they haven't left yet and my key is there and safe."

Claw didn't need to be told twice. She raced back toward Mr. Connor's yard with Emmy close behind.

Giselle heard a high-pitched cry in the distance. "Did you hear that? Sounded a little like Emmy."

"Nah, that wasn't our sister," replied Clare. "Maybe it was a bird?"

"This day keeps getting weirder," noted Giselle.

Clare nodded. "I don't see any missing snacks from my backpack," she said. "Let's go to the Paw Park. We can help Emmy, *and* figure out what kind of animal that was."

"And then warn our neighbors," added Clare.

The girls were beginning to get Fluffy's bag ready for the trip back when Claw burst into the yard.

"*Ahoo!*" went the bear.

"*Aroo!*" answered Fluffy.

"*Yip, yip, yip!*" went Soar as she beat her wings furiously.

Emmy rushed in, red in the face and breathing hard. "Help! I forgot it!" she gasped.

"What?" asked Giselle.

Emmy's eyes landed on the backpack. "The key! It was on the bag. My necklace must have fallen off when we rushed to get the Pet Cam out. Have you seen it?"

"No, but it's gotta be in the grass. Don't worry, sis. We were just packing up. We'll find it," Giselle assured her.

They dropped to their knees and scoured the grass for the shiny metal key on the ribbon. But it was nowhere to be found.

"You don't think . . ." began Giselle.

"Why would an animal take a key?" answered Clare.

"What are you talking about?!" demanded Emmy.

Clare told Emmy about the brown critter that had bolted across the yard, to the backpack, and then back into the woods.

"Oh no!" Emmy gasped. "That animal took my key!" She stared at the ground as tears slipped from her eyes.

"Em, don't cry," said Giselle.

Emmy looked at her sisters in disbelief. "I've abandoned the pets *and* lost the key to the clinic. Dad will be so disappointed in me!"

CHAPTER 15

Clare hugged Emmy tight. "Don't worry, Em. We're going to find the key."

Giselle looked toward the woods where the animal had disappeared. "Wait, I see something." She jogged into the forest, plucked something off a bush, and raised it in the air.

Emmy jumped to her feet. "What is it?"

Giselle returned with a strand of green

ribbon. But the rest of the ribbon, and the precious key, were nowhere in sight. Emmy looked like she might cry again. Clare put an arm around her shoulders. "Em," she said gently. "Here's a thought. You know, when I make a collage, I never know how it's going to turn out. But by trying different pieces in different places, I always end up with something fantastic."

Emmy looked at her sister. "Huh?"

"This may not be exactly the same, but I bet if we try putting the clues together in different ways, we *will* figure what kind of animal took the key. Then we can track the creature down!"

Emmy wiped her eyes. "Working together *is* our super power."

"Okay, so what do we know so far?" began Giselle.

"Our thief is an animal," noted Clare. "It was midsize and brown, and came out of the woods. We just saw him steal something. And he hissed! Miss Amaya heard that same sound when her garbage was ransacked."

"An animal probably gnawed the doorbell wires. And broke into the garbage and ate stuff," added Emmy.

"So it was hungry," Giselle concluded.

"Right," said Emmy. "But it also took the trash-can lids, the lightbulbs, and my brand-new key. You can't eat those—ugh! These clues just don't fit together."

Clare shifted as she thought. "Hmm . . . maybe the *hungry* part is what's throwing us off."

"What do you mean?" asked Giselle.

"Maybe the animal was attracted to the things it took for another reason."

"Okay," agreed Emmy. "So, what do the things have in common?"

The girls walked around the lawn. The items didn't seem related at all. But then Emmy sucked in her breath. "I can't believe I didn't think of this sooner! They're shiny!"

Giselle looked confused. "Come again, sis?"

"Think about it. Lightbulbs. Silver trash-can lids! And my metal key was brand-new—*super* shiny!" Emmy exclaimed.

"But what does that have to do with our thief?" asked Clare.

"Some birds and animals are curious about shiny things," said Emmy.

"So should we lay out more shiny stuff and wait for it to come back?" wondered Clare.

Suddenly Giselle grabbed Emmy's hand. "We don't need to! I just remembered another clue we found. C'mon. You gotta see this!"

Giselle led Emmy to the tracks the animal had left in the mud. Emmy dropped to her knees to examine them. Then she sat back on her heels and smiled. "Trills, I know who our bandit is!"

"Then spill, sis, spill!" said Clare.

"A raccoon! Raccoons are interested in lots of things, but shiny things in particular. Plus, they have a toe that works like a thumb on their front paw. It lets them twist, pull, and tear. A raccoon could have unhooked the straps on the trash cans *and* unscrewed the lightbulbs! And, I forgot: they are vocal, and can make hissing sounds." Emmy was so excited she jumped up and down.

"Wait. I'm still stuck on the shiny stuff. *Why* does it take those things? Sounds like a lot of work," noted Giselle.

"Maybe the raccoon just couldn't resist. I know all about liking shiny things," teased Clare. She jiggled her wrist, where she wore three bracelets made from mirrored beads.

"No one knows for sure, but the thought is the shine attracts their attention and curiosity. Raccoons are super smart," explained Emmy.

Giselle pulled her sister up. "You convinced me, Em. Our thief is a raccoon. Now we've just got to find him!"

"Hold up. Let me just make sure the pets are still okay." Emmy switched on the Pet Cam. The animals sat comfortably in their cages. She breathed a sigh of relief. Just a little more time away and she'd find the key. Then all would be well.

CHAPTER 16

The girls put Claw and Fluffy in their carriers and Soar on Giselle's shoulder and then followed the raccoon's tracks into the forest. The bushes and plants were thicker here. The sisters had to stoop low in some places, and step high in others to avoid the green that seemed to be growing everywhere.

"This is a workout, Trills, but we've gotta find this critter," Emmy said firmly.

"Can we pick up the pace?"

"Let's try," Clare replied.

Emmy didn't want to alarm her sisters, but every so often she glanced back. She couldn't see Mr. Connor's yard anymore, or any of the Trillizens' houses or tree houses for that matter. Nothing looked familiar. *What have I gotten us into? I can't let my father down, but I can't get us lost, either.*

"It feels like we've been following these tracks forever," complained Clare.

"Listen, I think I hear water!" said Giselle.

"We may be getting close, then," Emmy noted. "Raccoons like water. They can even swim! Their paws are more sensitive in water, and they use them to catch fish and frogs."

Sure enough, the ground began to slope, and the girls saw a stream running down the mountain. They splashed water on their faces and let the minis drink.

"The tracks stop here. Now what, detectives?" asked Giselle.

Emmy hopped across three flat rocks that made a path across the stream. Then she bent to examine the ground. "There are more prints on the other side. Come on!"

The girls didn't have to go much farther. The tracks ended at an old tree house that had clearly seen better days. There was a rickety set of stairs that led up the tall tree to the house. The glass for the front windows was long gone, the door was hanging on by a hinge, and there were holes in the roof.

"Whoa," said Giselle. "I wonder who lived here?"

"No clue, but it's abandoned now. This is a real fixer-upper," observed Emmy.

"But one person's trash is someone else's treasure. I bet the raccoon loves this place," Clare guessed.

"I'm going up," Emmy declared.

"Em," Clare began, "those stairs look wobbly. I'm not sure it's safe. Plus, what are the odds that you'll find the raccoon—*and* the key up there?"

"I don't know. But I've got to try." Emmy gingerly placed her foot on the bottom step. It creaked.

Giselle held up a hand. "I don't like this, and I'm not sure that Dad would either."

At the mention of her father, Emmy felt tears in her eyes.

"But that's why I have to find the key! I just *have* to," she repeated.

"Then I'm coming with you," Clare said.

Emmy took a deep breath. Her heart hammered as she forced herself to climb the stairs. The wooden planks shook each time she took a new step, but she made it up, and entered the old tree house. Clare grabbed the wobbly railing and followed her sister up and into the house.

From the ground, Giselle paced. *What should I do? Follow, or stay here in case help is needed?*

Clare and Emmy quickly looked around for the raccoon, but didn't see any evidence of him.

Then, suddenly, there was the sound of wood splintering. "Oh no!" Emmy cried out.

Down below, Giselle realized with a sinking feeling that the decision of whether to follow or stay had already been made for her.

CHAPTER 17

After a tremendous collapse, the stairs lay in a dusty pile on the ground.

Safe in the house, Emmy and Clare each raced to a window to look for another way down. There was nothing, and it was too high to jump.

"Emmm! Claaare!" Giselle shouted. "Are you okay?"

The minis ran in circles around the tree's

base, safely away from the wreckage.

"*Arooo!!!*" Claw howled.

"*Arf, arf!*" Fluffy barked.

"*Yiiiiip!*" went Soar.

And then, another loud *Crackkkkk!*

"NO!" Giselle gasped.

"What was *that* noise, Giselle?" called Emmy.

"The beams supporting the house. I don't know how much longer they'll hold. They are rotten and splitting. You have to get out!" cried Giselle.

Clare and Emmy starting brainstorming ideas for their escape.

Meanwhile, Giselle searched the outside of the tree house. "There, Trills!" yelled Giselle.

"What?" Clare called.

Giselle pointed to a large tree branch that was growing just outside the house. If the sisters leaned far enough out of the window, they could reach it and get out.

Clare didn't have to be told twice. She got onto the branch and scooched herself safely away from the rickety house. Then she wrapped both legs and arms around the branch as tightly as possible, bracing for whatever came next. "Em, c'mon!"

"I'll try," said Emmy. She reached carefully for the branch, but her nervous stomach flip-flopped again, harder this time. She shut her eyes and leaned back into the tree house. *Ugh! Now is not the time to be afraid!* she told herself.

It was as if her sister read her mind. "Don't think, Em. And don't look down! Just look at me. . . . Good. Now reach for the limb, and climb out," Clare encouraged.

Emmy leaned out the window and eased herself onto the same branch as Clare. She hugged the tree as hard as she could.

And it was just in time. The beams supporting the tree house had reached their limit. They gave way and there was a deafening noise as the whole house crashed to the forest floor. *BOOM!* The ground vibrated, causing the tree to shake.

"Aahhh!" cried Clare.

"Help!" screamed Emmy.

Giselle had jumped out of the way just in time. She looked up at her sisters, who had managed to hang on but were now dangling from the branch. They were too high up for Giselle to reach them, and also too high for the girls to safely drop down.

"Trills, stay strong!" she cried.

Clare looked down at Giselle and suddenly noticed a soft pink glow out of the corner of her eye. The pink petal charm that she wore as an earring tugged slightly away from her face. "Trills, are your charms activating?"

"I think so," Emmy answered. She could feel her green necklace charm lift off her chest and strain toward Clare's pink charm.

Pop! Pop! The charms shot out of the jewelry and hovered together in midair. Then, *zoom!* Giselle's blue charm whizzed out of her anklet and raced to meet the other two

charms. Together they formed one
large, seamless, glowing trillium-flower
charm!

Next the glimmering flower fired off a
massive burst of light. The whole forest

shimmered. And *Whoosh!* The mini'mals were transformed into a huge, strong bear; a wolf; and an eagle, and the sisters now wore warrior wear. The sun glinted off Giselle's lightning bolts.

"Yaaas! Perfect timing, as always!" Giselle cried. She jumped onto Soar. "Trills, I'm coming!"

CHAPTER 18

Once Giselle and Soar were in the air, she hesitated. Both Clare and Emmy were hanging onto the branch for dear life. Giselle couldn't get them both at the same time. Who should she save first? She had never had to choose between her sisters before.

"Get Clare!" Emmy called. "She's farther out, and that part of the branch is thinner and less sturdy."

"Okay, I'm coming!" Giselle cried. She steered Soar toward Clare.

Emmy's arms felt like lead weights. She was only holding on now through sheer will, but she couldn't let Giselle see her struggling. Giselle had to get their sister first.

"*Gotcha!*" Giselle grabbed Clare around the waist and pulled her onto Soar. "Em, you're next."

"O . . . kay," Emmy gasped. She didn't want to alarm her sisters, but she didn't think she could hold on long enough.

"*Ahoooo! Ahooooo!*" Emmy glanced down to see her now full-size bear running in circles below her. Claw was howling, and the force of her breath was whipping the leaves right off the ground like a leaf blower. Claw circled

faster and faster, creating a leaf pile as tall as herself.

My pet has a power, too! She can howl to make wind! That was Emmy's last thought before she lost her grip and felt herself falling through the air.

CHAPTER 19

"Ooompf!" Emmy landed on the ground. But instead of smacking hard soil as she had feared, she fell into something soft. *A pile of leaves! My bear saved me!*

"Emmmm!" Giselle shouted from up above.

"I'm okay—aahhh!" Though the leaves had softened Emmy's fall, the ground was sloped. Suddenly she rolled forward, and then started somersaulting down a hill that kept getting steeper and steeper.

"Trills, help!" cried Emmy. "I can't stop rolling!"

"We're coming," called Giselle.

Soar flew toward Emmy, with the two sisters on her back.

"*Ahoo!*" howled Claw. The brave bear raced down the mountain trying to reach her.

"*Aroo, roo, roo!*" Fluffy galloped down the slope, too.

"Faster, Soar!" Giselle commanded. But Emmy was way ahead of them. Emmy threw out her arms, clutching for something to slow her down, but nothing seemed to work.

While Giselle guided Soar, Clare could see her sister from the air, and called out to help her. "Em! Ahead of you. A tree. Watch out!"

Emmy was rolling right for the tree! She had to avoid it, but how? *My magic heals. I've closed cuts and made uprooted plants regrow* she thought to herself. *Wait . . . grow?*

Next to the tree was a large bush. If she timed things just right, could she make the bush grow big enough to protect her? She had to try. *Ready? Three, two, one, now!*

Emmy stretched as far as she could, and her hand grazed the bush. She felt a jolt, and then *Schwomp!!* The bush grew wider and wider until a thick leafy underbrush was directly in her path.

Emmy rolled into the bush. *Boing!* The bendy green branches cushioned her and bounced her back from the tree. She rolled slightly back uphill and came to a gentle stop.

"Em, are you okay?" Giselle called. Soar landed and the girls ran to their sister, just as

Claw and Fluffy reached her, too. The pets licked her all over.

"I think so," said Emmy. She hugged the animals, and then she stood up.

"Dancing Daisies!" Clare exclaimed. "That bush tripled in size. How did that happen?"

Emmy raised her hand in the air. "It seems

these magic powers of mine can do more than heal. I can make things grow, too."

Giselle gave her a high five. "Amazing!"

Clare winked. "Our pets' powers are growing, too. Did you see Claw howl to make wind? She's got magic bear air."

"That is downright pawsome!" exclaimed Emmy.

The girls giggled. It sure felt good to laugh after all they had been through.

CHAPTER 20

The group raced back up the hillside to the fallen tree house. As happy as they were to be safe and reunited, they had to remember why they were here in the first place. Emmy wondered, "Is it possible we missed spotting the key before the house came down? We were in a big hurry."

"Lemme check," said Clare. She trained her super vision on what remained of the tree house. While she still didn't see the key, her powers enabled her to notice some faint raccoon prints *behind* the tree.

"Where do the new tracks lead?" wondered Emmy.

"Only one way to find out," answered Clare.

"Uh-oh, Trills," Giselle said. She was holding the flower charm made from their three petals. They could see it was fading. And then, *Poof!* The glow flickered out completely. With that, the individual charms pulled apart. A moment later the girls were back in their regular clothes and the maxi'mals were mini'mals once again.

"Ugh," Giselle moaned. "This is no time

to lose our magic! We're so close to finding that key."

Emmy smiled confidently. "Trills, don't forget. We still have the best power of all, each other."

"Em's right. Sister power is mighty. Now, where could that raccoon have gone?" Clare said as she looked around.

Emmy followed her sister's gaze and saw the stream. "Clare, you're a genius!"

"I am?"

"Yes! You reminded me of the stream. Remember, raccoons love water—maybe that's where he went," Emmy said.

Emmy glanced at the sky. The sun was lowering. They had to get back to the clinic and bathe the pets before their owners returned for pickup. Emmy sprinted toward the stream. She knew this was their last chance.

CHAPTER 21

"You don't need super vision to see these tracks," Clare said as she approached the water.

"Someone has definitely been here," Giselle agreed.

"Someone definitely *is* here!" Emmy exclaimed. "Look!" She jutted her chin toward the stream where a raccoon was swimming through the water. "We found our bandit."

Clare laughed. "He really does look like a

bandit, with that stripe across his face."

"Now we just need to find the key," added Emmy. The girls searched along the stream and even peered into the water.

"I don't see it," said Clare.

"Me neither," said Giselle.

"It's gotta be here," Emmy insisted. "Let's look in the underbrush."

But just then, Claw nudged Emmy. She rubbed her snout into Emmy's leg.

"Not now, Claw. I have to find my key!"

"You might want to see what she wants," said Giselle. "That bear has been pretty help-ful today."

"You're right," agreed Emmy. She bent down, and her heart skipped a beat. Claw held a green ribbon in her teeth, and from the end dangled Emmy's precious key. "Claw! First the leaf pile that caught my fall, and now this! You beautiful, beautiful bear! You saved the day! What would I do without you?" Emmy scooped up Claw and hugged her tight.

"Trills, I would say this mystery is officially solved!" Clare cheered.

"Bull's-eye," agreed Giselle. "Now to the Paw Park. Pronto."

CHAPTER 22

As soon as they arrived at the clinic, Emmy used her key to open the door. Harry the bunny hopped up and down in his cage at the sight of them.

"Hi guys!" Clare said as she walked in. "We don't have much time before your owners come back. I say we do a group bubble bath in the big tub."

"Good idea," agreed Emmy. "That will be fun for these sweeties. Can you and Giselle get the bath started? There's something I need to do first."

"Sure," Giselle said. She and Clare took the pets from their cages and led them to the large metal tub. She turned on a gentle stream of warm water and poured in a drop of soap. Bubbles began to form, to the pets' delight.

Emmy retrieved paper and markers from the clinic desk and began to write. When she finished, she put the paper on a table by the tub and joined her sisters, who were already toweling off the clean pets. "What'cha got there, Em?" asked Clare.

Emmy held up her paper. She had drawn a raccoon on the top. There was a lot of writing underneath it. "Our customers need information about raccoons to make sure their things don't go wrong or missing again," she said.

"Huh, raccoons don't like garlic," Giselle said as she read the flyer. "I thought they ate everything! Who knew?"

"Who knew what?" asked Mrs. Heartlove as she walked into the Paw Pad.

"We figured out who took your things!" Emmy exclaimed. She handed her a flyer.

"I'm going to have to lock my garbage lids down even better. I didn't realize raccoons were so good with their paws," Mrs. Heartlove remarked.

Miss Amaya and Mr. Connor entered and took flyers, too.

"Trills, we can't thank you enough for today. I can tell the pets loved the Paw Park. Harry looks happy, super clean, and well fed," Mr. Connor observed.

"Whoa, what'd I miss?" Dr. J.A. asked as he walked in. The Trills' little brother, Zee, was with him, wearing a big backpack.

"Just that your daughters are the best," Miss Amaya added. She showed him the flyer. "They took great care of our pets, helped us with a problem, and provided this incredibly useful information!"

"I'm not surprised," Dr. J.A. said with a smile.

After the neighbors left, Dr. J.A. gathered his children. "So, how'd it go? Everything looks spic-and-span."

The girls exchanged a look. "Zee, little man, want to race in the Paw Park?" asked Giselle.

"Do I ever!" Zee cried. He ran down the stairs.

"Em, fill Dad in and we'll play with Zee downstairs," Clare suggested.

"Thanks, Trills," said Emmy gratefully. When they were alone, Emmy handed the key back to her dad.

"Em, you can keep this. For next time. I know I can count on you," Dr. J.A. said.

Emmy took a deep breath. She knew what she had to do. "Dad, today didn't go as smoothly as it might look."

"Looks like you handled it fine." Her dad smiled at her.

"No, there's more you need to know," insisted Emmy. "When our neighbors dropped their pets off this morning, they told us about mysterious things happening at their homes. They were missing things, too! We wanted to help, so we left the animals in their cages when they were napping to try to figure things out for them."

"Em, it's good to help your neighbors. I don't see the problem," said Dr. J.A.

"Well, we were gone a long time and we ran into some trouble," continued Emmy.

"Hmm. Maybe we should sit down." Dr. J.A. patted the couch next to him.

"Yeah," agreed Emmy.

Emmy filled her father in on everything. She told him how she lost the key when they'd been out trying to solve the mystery. She explained about the abandoned tree house and how they'd almost gotten hurt. When she was done, she could barely meet his eyes.

Dr. J.A. lifted his daughter's chin. "Em, you're a sensitive person. That's something I love about you. You feel for others and want to help them."

"That *is* why I decided to leave the pets at the Pad, Dad," Emmy agreed.

"With the Pet Cam, you made sure our furry friends stayed safe and had a fine day,"

said her father. "But," continued the doctor, "you should *not* have risked danger by going into that tree house, no matter what was missing."

"I know, Dad. I'm sorry," said Emmy. "I only went in because I was looking for the key. I didn't want to seem irresponsible."

"Em, *things* can be replaced. People can't. You and your sister's safety is more important than anything else."

"You're right, Dad. Now that I think about it, I should have just told you I lost the key. I won't do anything that risky again," agreed Emmy.

"Sounds good. And remember honey, everyone makes mistakes. Learning from them makes you a leader."

Emmy felt more peaceful than she had all day. The butterflies in her stomach were gone.

"Now, why don't we go find your sisters and brother," he suggested.

They walked down the stairs. The lights were out.

"Dad, what's going on?" Emmy wondered.

"Surprise! Happy Grand Opening!" her family members shouted as the lights turned on. They had arranged a picnic on the floor of the Paw Park with her favorites, daisy juice and strawberry shortcake.

"It was all in my backpack!" Zee said proudly. "Did I get ya, Emmy? Did I?"

"You sure did, Zee," agreed Emmy. She smiled from ear to ear. "I am so lucky to have all of you as my family."

"Funny, I was going to the say the same thing," said Dr. J.A. He opened his arms wide and Emmy fell in for a hug.

"Samesies," Giselle said as she joined the group.

"Ditto," added Clare as she squeezed into the center of the hug.

"Wait for me!" said Zee. He ran toward them, and Giselle picked him up.

When they had finished the cake and the daisy juice, Emmy sighed happily. "I wish we could stay in the Paw Park all night. It's like being outside, but we're inside!"

"I think your wish may come true," said Dr. J.A. with a twinkle in his eye. He ran across the garden and retrieved a duffle bag he'd stowed earlier that morning.

"Daddy, can I show them. Can I? Can I?" Zee bounced up and down.

"Go for it," said their dad.

Zee unzipped the duffle and pulled out five sleeping bags and pillows. Then Dr. J.A. dimmed the lights. With the mirrored ceiling and the softer light, it looked like there were a thousand stars overhead.

"No way!" exclaimed Giselle.

"This is incredible," agreed Clare.

"It's perfect," said Emmy.

As the lights glimmered, the family snuggled into their sleeping bags and the mini'mals cozied in between them. Then, Dr. J.A. pulled out a book and read them to sleep. It was a mystery, of course.

Photo credit: Carrie Leonard

Laura Brown is an early childhood expert and is currently Curriculum Director at Warner Bros. Discovery's preschool block, Cartoonito. She has served as Content Expert and Research Director for TV series at Nick Jr., Disney Junior, Amazon Kids, DreamWorks Animation Television, PBS Kids, Universal Kids, and many others. She lives in Tenafly, New Jersey.

Photo credit: Sylvie Rosokoff

Elly Kramer is currently the VP of Production & Development at Imagine Entertainment in their Kids & Family division. She has created and led the development of numerous award-winning TV shows, online games, and apps, and has produced and developed over thirty-five shorts. She lives in Los Angeles, California.